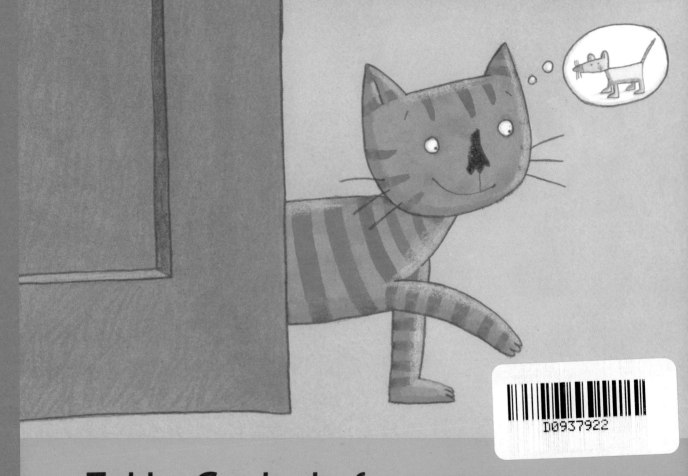

Tabby Cat looks for a mouse.

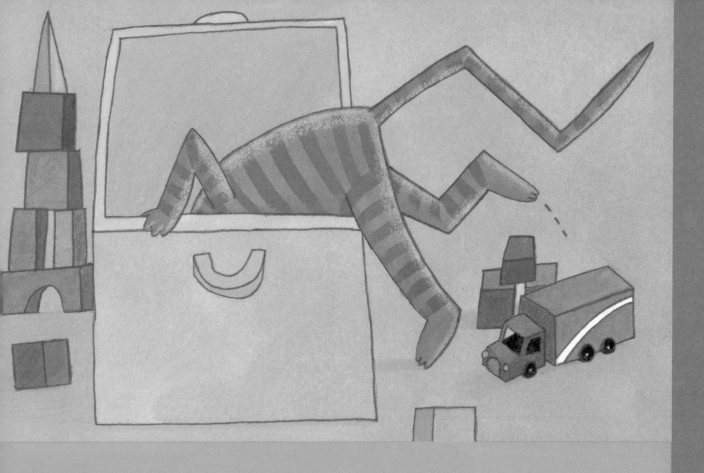

No mouse in the box.

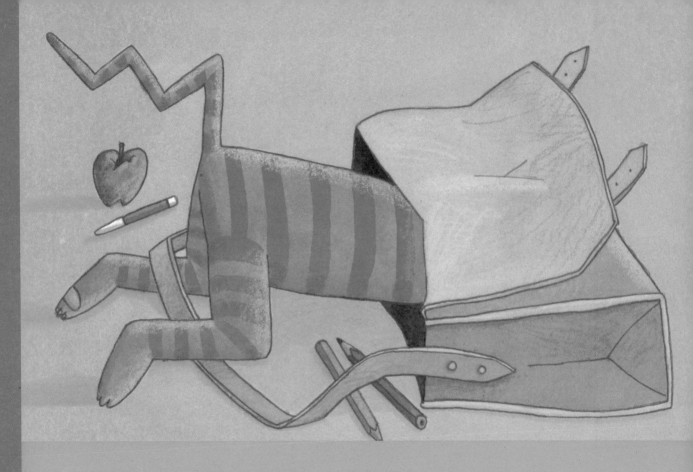

No mouse in the bag.

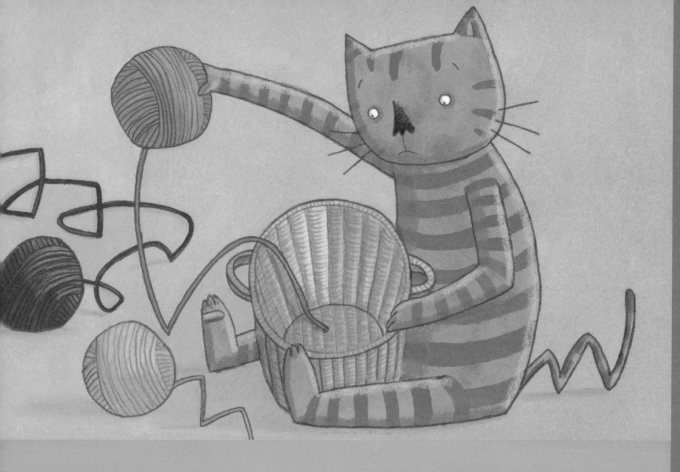

No mouse in the basket.

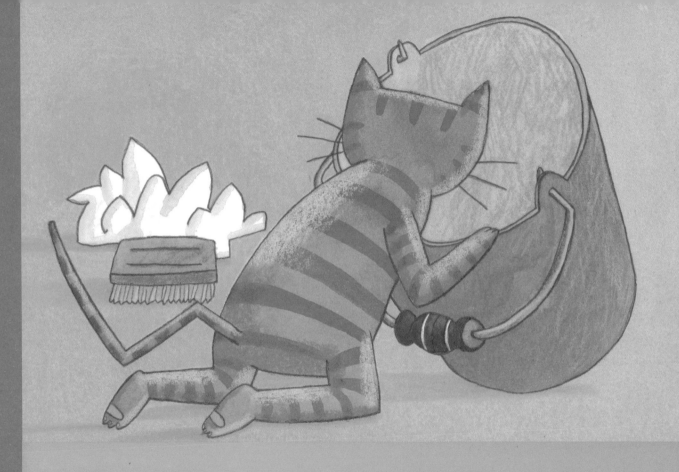

No mouse in the bucket.

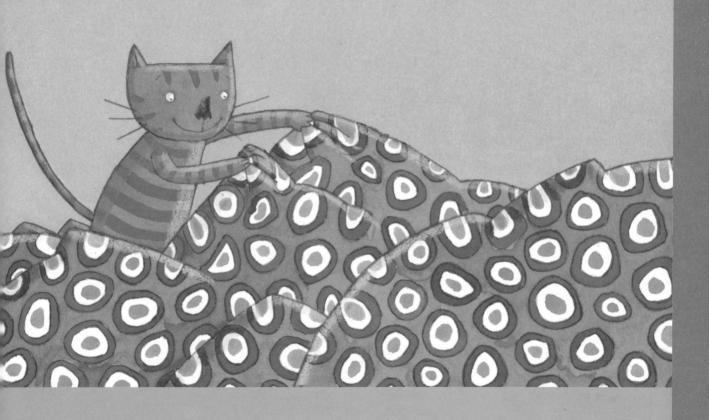

Look! A mouse under the blanket!

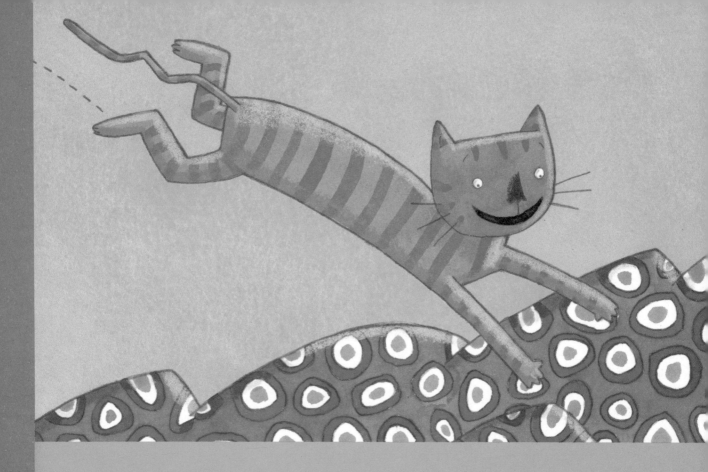

Tabby Cat jumps.

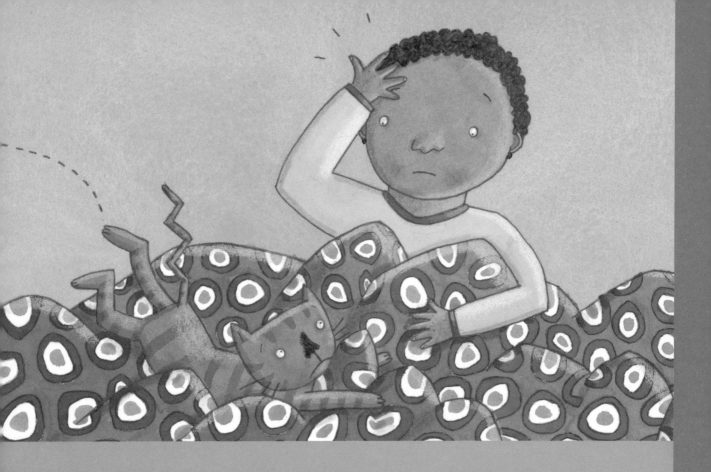

No mouse. "Ouch!" says Sammy.